MESSAGE FROM MARS

PARNIKA BAJPAI

NewDelhi • London

BLUEROSE PUBLISHERS
India | U.K.

Copyright © Parnika Bajpai 2025

All rights reserved by author. No part of this publication may be reproduced, stored in a retrieval system or transmitted in any form or by any means, electronic, mechanical, photocopying, recording or otherwise, without the prior permission of the author. Although every precaution has been taken to verify the accuracy of the information contained herein, the publisher assumes no responsibility for any errors or omissions. No liability is assumed for damages that may result from the use of information contained within.

BlueRose Publishers takes no responsibility for any damages, losses, or liabilities that may arise from the use or misuse of the information, products, or services provided in this publication.

For permissions requests or inquiries regarding this publication, please contact:

BLUEROSE PUBLISHERS
www.BlueRoseONE.com
info@bluerosepublishers.com
+91 8882 898 898
+4407342408967

ISBN: 978-93-7018-103-8

Cover design: The Revieree Studios
Typesetting: Namrata Saini
Editor & Illustrator: The Revieree Studios

First Edition: May 2025

Disclaimer

This is a work of fiction. Any names, characters, organizations, or events mentioned in this book are purely fictional. Any resemblance to actual persons, living or dead, or to real organizations or events, is entirely coincidental.

About the Author

Parnika Bajpai, also known as Jiya, is the youngest travel vlogger to host her own YouTube channel, Jiya-The-Explorer. At just 12 years old, she shares her passion for writing and traveling by documenting every place she visits through her vibrant vlogs. In addition to her love for exploring, Parnika is a talented public speaker and an active member of the Toastmasters Club, where she has won several public speaking competitions.

She is also an avid sports enthusiast with a particular passion for badminton. Parnika is known for her kindness toward her friends and deep respect for her teachers and parents. She dreams of becoming a successful author and has an extraordinary aspiration—to be the first person to set foot on Mars. With her love for space technology, she is determined to make this dream a reality.

Table of Contents

One: The Mysterious Noise 1

Two: A Glimpse of the Cosmos 7

Three: Countryside Planetarium 11

Four: The Midnight Message 20

Five: Goodluck Scientists 23

Six: A Sudden Departure 26

Seven: What's Special About April 31

Eight: The Unexpected Adventure 37

Nine: Turning Point in Jiya's Life 44

Ten: A Hurdle 49

Eleven: A Mysterious Discovery 57

Twelve: The Robot on Mars 63

Thirteen: The Collaborative Quest 67

Fourteen: Triumph and Recognition 74

Fifteen: Tick-Tock-Tick 82

ONE
The Mysterious Noise

"Good morning, Seattle. Today's most compelling news is going to shock you all. Astronomers have been researching Mars for weeks, and the most perplexing thing they've discovered is a cryptic message from the red planet. However, they haven't disclosed this jaw-dropping news to the public until they can fully understand it. That's all for today. We'll meet you tomorrow morning with something special." Dad switched off the TV, curiously scratching his head. He looked at Jiya calmly and gently, then asked, "Do you think what I think?" Both jumped with excitement, and the word "telescope" seemed to echo in the room.

Jiya and her family lived in the bustling city of Seattle, USA. She was a middle school student at Oxford Middle Schooler's Academy. Her dad was an astrophysicist, and his passion ignited

Jiya's interest in space. One summer evening when Jiya was four, as she was about to sleep, something twinkling in the sky caught her attention. She asked her dad, "Daddy! What's that in the sky?" He smirked and replied that it was a star. Little Jiya didn't understand, so in curiosity, she asked again, "Stir? But that's what you call mixing eggs and pudding for a delicious omelet for breakfast." He smiled at her innocence and said, "Oh dear! You have a good sense of humor, haha!" Jiya stared at her dad in frustration. "Are you going to explain it to me or not?" Dad said, "Okay, okay! So stars are celestial bodies that have been in the sky for ages. They're huge and made of gas. Each star is unique. Millions of years ago, some stars exploded due to excessive gas, and this universe was formed, including planets, the sun, asteroids, and galaxies. There are eight planets in our solar system: Mercury, Venus, ... and Neptune." That was the first time Jiya felt truly interested in something, so she decided to go camping every Sunday for stargazing. Dad agreed and planned it for the next day.

Their camping trips were incredible. At night, the stars sparkled, and through a telescope, they could see planets like Saturn, Jupiter, and Venus. *At midnight, the entire Milky Way shone brightly above their tent. Every week, Jiya wrote in her journal to record the wonders she experienced.*

Camping was Jiya's absolute favorite. It was a fixed part of her schedule, and she wouldn't miss it for anything. Even when her school organized an annual function and teachers asked her to participate in speech and solo dance (an honor usually reserved for smart and multitasking students), she declined to continue her camping routine.

Her love for astronomy was boundless. She was eager to explore life beyond our galaxy. Not a single day passed without her connecting with the stars. Astronomy fascinated her, and she and her dad immersed themselves in it every moment.

When the news about the message from Mars aired, they were both eager to solve the mystery. *Jiya exclaimed, "We're going to party tonight! I'm so excited to see the message from Mars. Daddy, from today, we're working on it. I've already named this project 'Mission: Message from Mars.' Are you with me?"*

Her father grinned. "Yes!"

That night, Jiya and her dad peered through the telescope that was attached to a radio signal receiver, searching for a signal from Mars. Neither blinked for a moment, consumed by curiosity. Days passed without any sign, and Jiya's enthusiasm waned. Jiya was determined to be the first person to decode a cryptic message from another planet. She stared at the stars every night, refusing to give up hope. If the world's greatest astronomers couldn't solve the mystery, maybe a fresh perspective, her perspective could make a difference. One day, she vowed, she would uncover the truth.

Then, she saw something blinking and sparkling from Mars. She zoomed in closely when suddenly the receiver turned on...it was a radio signal transmission! Dad quickly fed the signal into a translator and they heard an unknown language that astonished them. The noise seemed familiar, like a mix of Asian, North Pacific, and Russian languages. It said, "My family has been experiencing diseases, and the surface is decreasing day by day. No matter if we travel to another galaxy, my family is..." But then, Mom called them for dinner, interrupting their focus.

TWO

A Glimpse of the Cosmos

As they descended the stairs, both continued discussing the Martian message. At the dinner table, a delicious aroma wafted from the kitchen. Mom placed a covered pot on the table. Intrigued, they waited as she lifted the lid, revealing a pot of hot sauce spaghetti. She smiled, saying, "Liam and Jiya, don't worry, this is just a starter; plenty of food is coming. Enjoy this while I finish cooking."

They eagerly dug in as she left the room. When she returned with plates, bowls, and pots, they wondered aloud what the other dishes might be. The feast included white sauce pasta, sizzling olive pizza, and a chocolate lava brownie for dessert.

As they ate, Jiya and her dad resumed their discussion about Mars. Mom interrupted, "Oh, come on! I came in here happy, but you're ruining it with your stupid Mars talk. Since we're in a good mood, let's talk about Jiya's picnic at the planetarium." Dad agreed, "Jiya will have a blast at our country's biggest planetarium. In fact, it's her first picnic after lockdown, isn't it?" They chatted about the picnic, and that night, Jiya fell asleep dreaming of the fun to come. The next morning, Jiya jumped out of bed and rushed to her mom. "Yay, Mommy! It's my picnic day! Can you pack me a grilled cheese sandwich, a chocolate muffin, and fresh fruit.

Soon, her bus arrived. Jiya, wearing a neat uniform and carrying a small bag with a water bottle, waved goodbye to her parents. She held a ticket with the planetarium's name and their signatures. "Mom, Dad, I'll miss you! Wish me luck for my first picnic. I'll take care of myself like you do. Bye!" Her parents waved goodbye with tears of joy. As the bus pulled away, they watched their daughter climb the steps with a big smile.

On the bus, Jiya sat by the window with her friends Suzy and Fiona. Suzy had long curly hair and was tall, while Fiona was shorter with short hair and bangs. Jiya was friendly with everyone. After a while, the bus stopped at the base of a mountain, and the teacher explained they would be trekking to the planetarium. Everyone was excited about the hike. They started walking, and Suzy complained about being tired. Fiona reassured her they would arrive soon. After a thirty to thirty-seven-minute hike, they saw a sign: "COUNTRYSIDE PLANETARIUM!" in large, bold letters. A smaller sign below indicated it was Seattle's largest planetarium. Everyone was amazed, and little did Jiya know this visit would be a turning point in her quest to decode the Martian message.

THREE

Countryside Planetarium

As soon as they had a view of the outside board, their teacher requested them to move inside the planetarium. Everyone started sauntering after they were done gossiping about the planetarium inside. "Wow! This is a fairy tale... I can't believe it, guys," commented Fiona after stepping inside it. In fact, Fiona was totally right, it was a splendid view for all the students and the teachers. There was a huge dome screen after stepping one step ahead itself, and it was covered in navy blue background along with stars shining above them. Also, all eight planets were hanging on the ceilings for decor, the ones that were tall enough would bump into the planets and one of them got exasperated so he angrily said, "I am so over this, it's bumping every time I'm walking. Let me get down on my knees and spare my poor head." Everyone chuckled and after all it was done they continued their journey.

After a small stroll they all were able to see a glimpse of the radio transceiver, their teacher explained about the usage of it and spoke a few sentences on it. However, Jiya didn't pay attention to what her teacher was expounding, instead, she was so fascinated by it, that her intentions started speaking to her mind, "Hey Jiya! You should go inside and get a better look at the radio transceiver, and you might able to get some ideas for decoding the message from Mars. Now it's up to you, if you want to solve the message or be an ordinary student, just exploring the planetarium and returning back home with nothing to decode the message." Jiya was left dumbfounded and dicey about her intention's plan.

Ultimately she pondered and went through the plan her intentions initiated. Bravely snuck away from the crowd towards the radio transceiver room. There was no one to stop her as everyone's attention was on the teacher and the teacher was busy explaining, so Jiya could easily abscond from there towards the radio signal room. With a brave heart she proceeded into the room, but suddenly felt that someone was walking behind her and noticed a shadow had formed on the ground. For a second she stopped breathing and felt like a mini heart attack hit her body. She took a moment, sighed and slowly turned back.

To her surprise, "Hola, como estas! Are you heading towards the radio transceiver? Well in that case you should take the permission of your teacher my fellow, cause we scientists don't allow the kids here. Understood?" One of the Spanish scientists said to Jiya. Jiya hesitatingly answered, "Ho-hola! I did take the per-permission from my teacher, dear sci-scientist." Then the scientist opened the door for her and led her inside the room. She looked at the 360 degree angle of the radio transceiver. She went a bit closer to it and started to question the scientist on how it worked but right then the scientist began to leave the room. At that moment, the teacher was nearly done, speaking on the last point, "So now, last but not least, this part below the radio transceiver is called the... Jiya?" One of the students interrupted, "Ma'am it's an antenna, not Jiya our friend. Ha ha ha!"

The teacher said, "OMG! That is Jiya, but how did she get in there? Children, you all wait here, I will come in a minute." The teacher rushed to the room and when Jiya noticed she was coming, she immediately hid behind the radio transceiver hoping she would not be caught. The teacher angrily exclaimed, "Jiya, there is no need to hide from me because I already caught you. Come show your face now!" Slowly Jiya got up and faced her teacher. She was extremely sorry for what she had done and apologised to the teacher.

Slowly she went to a room where a burst of knowledge would be grasped by the children because they had come to a planet zone (where there is plenty of information about all planets). Everyone was keen on whatever they were being shown, however, Jiya was still wondering about the radio signal and couldn't remove that picture from her mind. With that mindset, she thought of another plan. She grabbed Suzy's hand and pulled her towards the corner of the room. Suzy murmured, "What is going on, where are you taking me Jiya?" Jiya told her that she was taking her to the radio transceiver so that she wouldn't get scolded by the teacher for being alone. Suzy nodded her head in disbelief.

They had just arrived in the room when Suzy got a bit alarmed and pretended to run, but Jiya grabbed her hand tightly and stared at her furiously. Then they entered it and to their surprise, all the scientists were functioning the radio transceiver. Both of them thought twice about going inside but didn't know which step to take next, Soon they decided to take a risk, and in no time they asked the scientists to show the radio transceiver in action. "I'm sorry to tell you that the transceiver is currently unable to tune its system to receive any message from a planet, and also, we don't allow the children to step inside here. So without saying another word...please leave" Said one of the scientists. However, a twist of events took place while talking to the scientists that nobody could have anticipated. Was that a Zombie Apocalypse, Corona return or a natural disaster, that none of the scientists could have ever dreamed of?

Beside the radio signal, there was a T.V. kept. Near that, a scientist was examining the opposite parts of the radio transceiver when his eyes fell on the T.V and he was left astounded. Since the volume was extremely low, the scientists and the kids present on the other side were unable to hear it. He shouted out, "Guys you all will be completely wide-eyed after hearing me. Guess what, the message that we heard last night from Mars was fake! Basically, the news said that some people were sending a satellite near Earth to trick us into believing a creepy messages from Mars which would make those people famous and they would become rich. That means all our time and effort was left in the mud, and those grifters were earning money by committing fraud!" Everyone's jaw dropped in disbelief.

In a short time, Jiya spoke in excitement, "Oh yes! My dad and I just heard the message yesterday night too and we heard the exact same lines. Also, my dad taught me alot about radio signals, so if you allow me I can examine the radio signal and accordingly I can fix it." All the scientists looked at each other in such a manner trying to figure out the current situation. Then they nodded with slight smiles on their faces. Jiya understood their approval so she approached the radio transceiver and started looking at it carefully. In no time, Suzy patted Jiya on her back and when she turned around, unexpectedly her teacher was at the door with a frown on her face. Both Jiya and

Suzy were unable to decide the next step they should take, as in front of them their strict teacher was standing.

"This is enough, Jiya! First you went alone and now to save yourself from being caught, you took Suzy with you. And Suzy you too helped her... Both of you, go sit in the corner until this picnic ends. GO, NOW!" Shouted the teacher. Both of them got scared and did as their teacher said. After sitting down, Suzy sighed and questioned Jiya, "Jiya! Can you tell me what message you and other scientists were discussing? It all went over my head." Jiya looked at her and ignored her question and instead asked, "Suzy, because of me you got punished, and you will not be able to explore the planetarium but still you didn't get upset or angry with me?" Suzy smirked and hugged her tightly, "Oh come on! You're my best friend, and I am here to support you in any situation even if we both have to climb Mount Everest. I only want you to be with me forever so we both can face the hardest problems in life. So there is no need to get angry with you." Jiya felt mirthful, and she too hugged her bestie.

"Come on, children, it's time to go back home, let's trek 3 km again..." Called a voice from behind. Jiya and Suzy knew it was their teacher, so they stood up with their little bags on their shoulders. Suzy probed, "But Jiya, you still didn't answer my question, what message were you and other scientists were discussing?" Soon, she explained the entire story to Suzy, and when she finished, Suzy nodded and thanked Jiya. However, it seemed as if Suzy also wanted Jiya to include her in her plans. Jiya clearly understood and invited her into her plans as well. Her best friend jumped in excitement for being chosen. It showed 9 p.m. in the watch, when Jiya jumped off her bus and in front of the bus her house was there so she ran back home. Both the parents embraced her as a sign of love. Jiya said, "I missed you both so much! And do you know what happened? So..." She narrated the entire tale to her parents, leaving them stunned. Shortly, something stroked her mind that made her run to her room, as she came to her room Jiya asked her dad to come along too. "Whoa! What is that?" Dad exclaimed when Jiya pointed at something.

FOUR

The Midnight Message

When Jiya pointed at something, Dad decided to look through the telescope for a clearer view. Jiya agreed, and they carefully removed the telescope's cover, sending a cloud of dust into the room. Both peered through the telescope, but just as they were about to adjust the focus, Mom called out for dinner, interrupting their observation. Dad pleaded for more time to examine, but Mom firmly replied, "No means no! I knew you were both eager to use the telescope, so I gave you five extra minutes, but that time is up, and the food is getting cold. Come eat like good children." With disappointed faces, Jiya and Dad sat down to eat.

Suddenly, Mom smiled mysteriously. Jiya asked, "What's that smile for? Don't hide anything from me." Mom chuckled, "Well, your dad and I have a surprise for you. It might fulfill your dreams. Liam, should I tell her?" Dad nodded and led Jiya to a room where the gift was waiting. "Jiya, make space for your new radio receiver!" Mom announced. Jiya's eyes widened in excitement. Her dad carefully placed the new and upgraded radio signal in the room. "Can I listen to it now, please?" Jiya begged, but her parents suggested waiting until morning. Disappointed, she settled into bed with her teddy bear after her parents said goodnight.

Later, around 2:00 AM, a strange noise woke Jiya up. She wondered if her parents were awake and making the sound. After checking and finding them asleep, she realized the noise was coming from her room. Searching for the source, she finally discovered the new radio receiver emitting an intriguing sound. "Mom, Dad, come quick!" she shouted.

Her parents rushed in, startled by her sudden call. Jiya explained the situation. Dad listened carefully to the radio signal. Jiya suggested it might be another fake message, but Dad remained focused. The radio receiver suddenly vibrated and produced an unfamiliar sound. Both listened intently, and then, a shocking realization dawned on them.

FIVE
Goodluck Scientists

The sound abruptly vanished. Jiya exclaimed, "Oh no! How can we decode the message now, Daddy?" Her dad was deep in thought when Jiya patted his shoulder, snapping him out of it. "Well, Jiya, I was wondering if we should seek help from someone. It would be easier, right?" Jiya agreed, "Who are we going to call this late at night?" Dad exclaimed, "Scientists!" Jiya's eyes lit up. "I know some scientists who are available 24/7. The ones we met at the planetarium were professionals. Let's go to the planetarium now; they might still be working." Without hesitation, Dad took Jiya to the garage and started the car. Excited, Jiya buckled up in the back seat.

After half an hour, they arrived at the planetarium, hoping to find the scientists. As they approached the radio signal room, a security guard spotted them. "You're trying to rob this place, huh? Robbers usually come at night, but I won't let you steal anything here.

Get out!" the guard yelled. Dad explained calmly, "We're here to meet the scientists about a message. We are not robbers, we need to talk to the scientists now, its important." The guard apologized and let them pass.

They found the room where the scientists were working.

Jiya burst in, explaining their situation. The scientists listened intently and agreed to help. However, they asked Jiya and her dad to leave due to the late hour. They promised to contact them if they made any discoveries. Disappointed but understanding, Jiya and her dad left the planetarium.

Back home, Mom asked about their meeting and if they had decoded the signal. Dad explained the situation, and they went to bed. The next morning, Dad's phone rang loudly, waking everyone up. Jiya rushed to their room, eager to hear the news. Unfortunately, it was Dad's boss calling about work. Jiya's excitement turned to disappointment as she realized they wouldn't be notified about any discoveries. With no clues about the mysterious message, silence filled the house.

SIX

A Sudden Departure

After Dad had left for his office, Jiya got into an extreme level of thinking that left her zoned out. Mom interrupted, "I can understand this situation is a building block for your successful future, but don't take it so seriously that you become unaware of your surroundings. Also, don't take my suggestion in the wrong way, it's not like I'm forcing you to stop thinking about such a massive thing. Instead, you should think about it, but also focus on other important things, like brushing your teeth and taking a bath now. So please, go do your chores." Jiya paid attention to what her mother said and followed as she said. She took a soft towel of anime characters and hung it on her shoulders, pretending to go to take a bath, but she instead called her dad's phone from inside the bathroom.

Her dad unfortunately didn't pick up the call. She got angry and scowled. At the same time, her dad had got a call from the scientist. He picked up the call and spoke, "Jiya you know right, that I'm in the office right now. Please don't disturb me." The other side of the call (meaning the scientist) answered, "Umm, I'm not Jiya, Mr. Liam. I'm the scientist (Mrs. John) you met, actually I came with the report. I'm sorry to say but, we tried till each drop of our sweat dripped. Unfortunately, we didn't receive any sort of signal." Dad got sad and ended the call in sorrow. He was about to share the message with Jiya and he even typed the whole message, when his boss called out in anger, yelling that he couldn't send the message to her.

However, on the other hand, at Jiya's house, she hit her heart deeply and her brain stopped working, all her hair follicles rose slightly and she got a little-painful goosebump in her arm. She said, "Wait a second! This always happens when one of my close-one is in grief. I think the one who can be in grief now, is my dad, as the scientist..." Her mouth stopped immediately and she sobbed loudly. Mom came and asked why she was sobbing. Jiya exclaimed, "Mom, my future will not be successful." Mom realised why she was saying that, so she called her dad in order to make her stop thinking about it. Soon in no time, her dad picked up the call and decided to leave the office and directly come back home. He got worried too, but decided to do anything for his daughter.

His daughter couldn't stop her tears until her dad showed up, looking very tired. He taught a lesson to his daughter in a very sweet manner, "See, since the scientist couldn't receive any message, it does not mean that your entire life is over. This situation is not the end of your life. Now you've a whole 90 years left, how difficult would it be for you to achieve your goal? And I'm 101% sure that the message will come anytime tomorrow or day-after-tomorrow, so have some patience. You know, Bill Gates once said, 'Patience is the key to success.' It clearly means that you have a lot of time. Some things have to take more time to come but patience will guide you to its gateway in a very easy way. So I believe you're now strong enough to face even bigger obstacles like this, right Jiya?" She wiped her tears off and smiled in encouragement. Jiya sighed, "Yes daddy, you are completely right!" Three of them hugged tightly together as if their problem was over and they now have nothing to be tensed about.

This moment of happiness was now over, when one of mom's friends' call came. She answered the phone. Both the fellows outside were in bewilderment, they scratched their heads and looked at each other. Jiya questioned, "Who could it be now, I hope it's not your angry boss who wants to bring you to office again." Dad smirked, "How could it be my boss on your mom's phone. It might be someone else, like her close friends, they call every now and then." Jiya nodded, in total agreement. Soon mom came out of the room looking at the two in stress and extreme tension.

She quickly went inside another room grabbing a huge suitcase. Both of them again felt fishy about mom doing weird stuff. Jiya went inside that room and saw her mom was packing everyone's clothes in that suitcase.

Her mom immediately went to dad and asked him to book three tickets for New Jersey. Before her dad could question, mom had gone outside with a cab waiting. She shouted, "Leave the house and come quick! We can book tickets for the flight at the airport. For now, just, come!"

SEVEN

What's Special About April

As soon as they sat in the car, Dad asked Mom desperately, "What is wrong with you? Can you now please tell the matter? Because, it seems to be something serious as you're telling us to leave the house, and shift to New Jersey." Mom spoke, "Actually my friend Niola, the astronomer, called and said that according to her reports, an asteroid was supposed to crash tomorrow in Seattle. So she told us to leave the house and go somewhere far.

I know, everything happened so quickly that there was no time to tell you guys. By the way, have you booked the tickets? If not, do it now, at the speed of light!" Both of them got slightly scared after hearing such extreme news. Dad booked the tickets for the three of them, and near him, Jiya got excited a bit.

The parents were shocked to see their little one getting hyper in such devastating news. Her mom asked Jiya, "Why are you looking so excited? It's not your birthday, silly!" Jiya excitedly answered, "An asteroid is going to crash near our house, wouldn't that be an opportunity of receiving the signal again? I mean there might be chances, and this time we will gather all our teammates, that will help in decoding it." Mom and Dad were looking in agreement but until then, they had boarded their flight and were off to New Jersey. "Now how will we be able to go to our house, wait till night, call everyone and decode the signal? Also, going somewhere where an asteroid is going to crash will be extremely dangerous and no-go!" Dad exclaimed in horror. Jiya was looking unbothered about what Dad was saying and instead yawned as if she didn't have any interest. Before the flight took off, she grabbed her phone and called Suzy.

She told Suzy the reason for calling and asked her to meet in New Jersey. Then she immediately dialed the scientists, but the flight attendant requested her to put her phone on flight mode as they were about to take off. She had done everything in a flash, and there was no time for her parents to question. After all that work, she uttered in relaxation, "Daddy, all what you were concerned about is now solved by your precious and multi-talented daughter! Now let me relax. By the way, do you know a perfect kids movie for me? That I can watch on the TV now, ooh, I got one already, 'Barbie!!!'" Both the parents were proud of having such an brilliant kid. Their flight landed in the biggest airport in New Jersey after a long five hours. Three of them got off the plane and stretched their bodies completely. Dad asked Mom, "So, I hope you must have decided where we should live for the next two days. Haven't you?" Before Dad could finish his question, Mom interrupted, "Yes, I have. You need not to worry. My friend Niola lives here itself. She has sent the address, until then let me book a cab." After a short period of time, the cab arrived and they settled down. Jiya got a conference call from the scientists and her bestie Suzy. After picking up the call, Suzy asked, "Well, we all have come to New Jersey, so are you ready to rock?" Everyone was filled with excitement and they screamed, "Yes, we are ready!" After all this, Jiya's parents called her to get down as they had reached Mom's friend Niola's house.

The house was very massive and seemed to be from the Queen Elizabeth era (old, vintage, and pretty fancy). After admiring the house from outside, they went near the main door and rang the doorbell. Someone answered the door; happily, it was Mrs. Niola herself. Mom hugged her tightly, and Niola returned the embrace. They were long-distance friends who had met physically after two years. Niola invited them inside and offered the adults cups of cold coffee and the little one, fresh watermelon juice along with some fries. Mom spoke up, "So, aren't you ready with all the equipment we need to use for the night to observe the crashing of the asteroid and Mars signals?" Niola happily answered, "Yep! But for now, you forget about those things and come with me. I'll give you a house tour. And Jiya, you too can join us, come let's go!" Jiya excitedly said, "Okie, dokie! Aunty Niola, since when I landed here, I was so eager to explore your house, and it seems to be very unique and fascinating already." After exploring the house and engaging in some gossip, night fell.

Mom proceeded towards the bedroom and asked if all the equipment was ready. Niola nodded but added, "What's the hurry, my dear? It's just 8 o'clock, and you know..." She seemed hesitant. Jiya mentioned that she had already called her friends, and they were arriving soon. Then Niola confessed, "See, the reason I'm doing this will shock you. I was just joking. The asteroid will not crash.

Happy April Fool's Day to you, he he ha ha...!!!" Mom, Jiya, and Dad's jaw-dropped, and there was complete silence for a moment, but Niola continued laughing.

EIGHT

The Unexpected Adventure

Soon, someone was at the door, ringing the doorbell loudly. Jiya thought of peeking through the peephole. To her surprise, it was Suzy and her parents waiting for someone to answer the door. Jiya exclaimed, "Mrs. Niola, it's my friend whom I called. Now what should I say in front of her, that it was all a prank, huh?" Jiya's dad answered, "Now that she has come, just open the door; at least we'll tell her what happened, no need to run away from the situation." Jiya nodded and answered the door. As soon as she opened the door, Suzy started chattering, "I got my telescope and along with that, all plans are done. Oh yes, most importantly, thank you, Jiya, for informing us before the asteroid could crash or else we could have died already." Jiya sighed and told both Suzy and her parents about the prank.

The three of them were left astounded and frustrated as they wasted both their time and money on such a silly thing. Niola apologized and felt sad for fooling them. She then spoke up, "Actually, the reason for my prank was not to make you all upset. It was to invite my best friend [Jiya's mom] to my house as I thought if I could have said it directly, she would have refused to come by making up some excuses.

That is why I had set up such a plan to invite you and your family to my house for some days." Mom looked at her innocence and understood her compulsion. She said, "Niola, there was no need to do all such things, and you know why? Yesterday Liam told me that we can plan to go on a vacation sometime now. It had been ages since we've been on a vacation, so we decided this. That's until your phone came, and we canceled our plan." Niola was in a great shock but then exclaimed, "I have a great idea! Now since you all are brought up here, why not let me give you a tour of New Jersey and you can have a vacation now? Right?" Everyone glanced at her and got excited.

However, Mom and Dad had one problem as they didn't bring enough clothes for a vacation, so they got a bit tense. Niola told them that they could go shopping and buy clothes immediately.

In no time, Jiya and Suzy walked towards their parents, and Jiya asked, "Mom, Dad, and Suzy's parents, will it be okay if we all together go to explore New Jersey? I mean, it was not worth coming all over here, but it can be now if we spend some memories together. I hope you all agree to my opinion, and Suzy too wants this. Please, pretty please..." The four agreed and took their bags to go shopping. Jiya and Suzy joined them by sitting in the back seat of the car.

"Woah, I've never seen such a tremendous mall in my entire life!" Jiya and Suzy exclaimed, stretching their necks up to view it from top to bottom. They entered and rushed to complete their main task, 'Shopping!!!' After an hour, each one of them came near the food court with at least two heavy bags in each hand. Then everyone ate some snacks in the food court and soon left the mall with joyous smiles. They drove to Niola's home back and rested for a while after that exhausting day. Niola sighed, "Guys, I think we rested for a long time now. Let's start by figuring out where to go tomorrow." Mom said, "Excuse me, Niola, you have been staying in this city for so many years so, you should know somewhere special to take us tomorrow, right?" "Well, I sure do!" said Niola. She decided to give them a surprise by taking them to the biggest indoor water park in New Jersey.

The next day, Suzy and Jiya woke up very early in the morning, as they were extremely excited to go outside and explore special destinations in this massive state. But what they did not know was, Aunty Niola had planned a surprise to take everyone to Dreamworks Water Park (biggest water park there). After some time, everyone woke up and packed their bags, being uncertain of where Niola was taking them. After everyone asked her a million times, Niola's ultimate answer was, "That... is... a... SURPRISE!" Well indeed, she was a good surprise-keeper. Suzy whispered to Jiya from the back, while everyone was keeping their luggage in the car trunk, "Psst, Jiya... I have a blockbuster idea to get to know where aunty Niola is taking us to? Let's check her phone; she might have asked Google Maps how far the destination is. I'm sure the Google Map's history will show the destination, and finally, our eagerness and excitement will cool down, what do you say?" Jiya was a bit worried but finally agreed.

They immediately went to search for Aunty Niola's phone. Jiya pointed, "I found it!" They tip-toed near it, but suddenly a voice cried from behind, "Ha, ha, ha... Are you serious guys, trying to disclose the surprise? Aww, I am so sorry, but that was a fake phone and the real one is in my pocket. I think you should get back in the car. Too much fun going on, huh?" They got back in the car acting innocent as if they didn't do a thing. Soon, Jiya's parents and Suzy's parents sat in the car when Niola started to drive. After some time, they reached their destination, 'The Dreamworks Water Park!!!' Everywhere, water, big and colorful water slides, and some of the Dreamworks characters like Shrek and Kung Fu Panda were waiting to invite them inside. It was a chaos of excitement shed in every corner, along with that, everyone's reaction was breathtaking. Niola exclaimed, "What's that waiting for? Let's get in and enjoy!" The group's faces were overflowed with joy and delight after reaching inside one of the castles in some fairytale movie.

However, that joyful smile and excitement were a bit hidden in Jiya's mom's face. She questioned, "Wow, Niola, thanks for bringing us here, but since we came to a waterpark, we too need some extra swimming costumes and I came wearing a t-shirt and jeans, how can we go dive inside now?" Niola perceived what she asked, but at the same time was clueless about what to do. Thankfully, Jiya saved their trip from coming to an end, as she had packed all sorts of clothes like: woollen, cotton, raincoats, and swimsuits for everyone because she didn't know where her aunt would take them, but she surely knew that there might be a perplexion of what to wear. She said, "Aunty Niola could have taken us to a mountain, some unique evergreen forest, or an amusement park, so I packed all the clothes in an emergency, so everyone, please wear your swimsuits and let's go have a splash!"

Every single person adored her intelligence, and within two minutes, they strolled off for their first ride. One hour later, they met at a main point where they could feast after all the fascinating but, a bit exhausting rides. After they were done with all the rides in the water park, Jiya exclaimed, "Thank you, Aunt Niola, for taking us to this Water park. It was a very blissful day today." Everyone pointed and agreed with the same thing that Jiya said.

They then left the water park with lots of encouraging memories in their minds. Suddenly, Jiya's dad excitedly called her, "Jiya come here, look what the board says..." There was a big board right in front of the water park, it was highlighted with blue and only blue. Jiya felt astonished until she read what was written; she too gasped in disbelief.

Suzy approached the board with wide eyes and jaw dropped, this meant she was enlightened with awe and was undoubtedly astounded. The others who didn't read the board were waiting for the taxi, but until then, Suzy spilled the beans to everyone by taking them towards it. The board was a turning point for Jiya's life ahead.

NINE

Turning Point in Jiya's Life

The attractive board everyone's eyes fell upon displayed the letters "A, R, I, M!" - a strange code. Below it, a short paragraph captured everyone's attention:

"Crack the code and help us solve the message, and you'll be rewarded with an internship at NASA! You'll even get to open your own space program, even a kids' program where you'll be the leader! So, wake up tomorrow with the exciting thought of unraveling the message and the code we've found. Best of luck! From the astrologers."

Little Jiya, of course, accepted the challenge. Encouragement bloomed in her eyes. Mom however, questioned, "Are you sure, Jiya? This could be a fraud. Let's agree never to read such suspicious advertisements again—" Jiya interrupted, "Well, Mom, if it were a fraud, wouldn't the astrologers not have included their symbol at the end of the poster?" Each astrologer's symbol was indeed present, suggesting they weren't fraudulent. After much discussion on their way back to Niola's home, they arrived, their minds still filled with confusion. Although Jiya was very interested, she too had some doubts that lingered in her mind.

As soon as they arrived, Niola brought a large tray with everyone's water glasses. While handing them out, Jiya's eyes caught a white twinkle shining from the antenna. She rushed towards it, causing her glass to fall and shatter. Niola followed, curious about Jiya's sudden movement. Jiya strained her eyes towards the stars, searching for any signal. Niola reached the antenna just as the door slammed shut and locked from the outside. The loud bang sent Jiya crashing to the floor in shock. Niola rushed in, screaming in panic.

The six people in the living room heard their screams and raced upstairs to investigate. To their surprise, the doorknob of the antenna room had suddenly come loose. The two trapped inside witnessed a shimmering, powerful, and captivating light that forced them to focus on the radio signal it generated, neglecting everything else.

The weather outside turned cold, with lightning flashing through the windows as rain began to pour. The peaceful breeze morphed into strong, harsh winds. The radio receiver then identified a distant star, and a signal began to emanate from it. Both Jiya and Niola smiled faintly, relieved to receive a signal.

Since Jiya was a radio signal expert, she started fiddling with some of the complex machine's simpler components. After some struggle, she managed to extract a phone-like device. Over the thunderous roar, she shouted to her aunt, "Aunty Niola, this is a translator that can translate the signal we just received! We just need to put the signal into it and wait patiently for it to translate. But Dad told me to stay away from this device. The signal power might be very strong, like a really high voltage, and could cause a dangerous blast that could severely injure us. So, are you ready? Let's finally end this suspense we've been waiting for months for!"

Niola nodded in horror. Taking five steps back, they both placed the device within the signal's reach.

The translator began translating the signal into English. Outside the window, strange storms were brewing. Niola started to move towards the window to close it, but Jiya stopped her. "No, no, don't close the window! The translator won't work if you do. The signal needs to catch the natural power for it to function." Aunt Niola asked her, "But how can we stay safe from this storm? We still can't escape the antenna room since the doorknob is broken, and we can't close the windows. We need a way out, or this storm could take our lives as well. Think, Aunty, think!" Dark, ragged clouds blanketed the sky. Thunderstorms crackled with an eerie menace. The harsh winds howled with a terrifying ferocity, and the storm grew bigger and bigger...

TEN

A Hurdle

A strange voice came from the translator when Jiya was talking to Aunty Niola, prompting what to do next. She bent down to her knees and crawled on the way to the translator. As she approached the device, she saw the window's glass falling down into pieces, which meant that the wind was strong enough to break the glass.

Jiya now found it very difficult to bring the translator as the wind and water falling on the device could electrocute her. Minutes passed after thinking and thinking, Niola stood near the door and shouted, "We both are stuck here, now we can't find a way to get out, guys help us out in whatever you can do. We beg you, please-eeeee!"

Meanwhile, the other six who were outside were thinking for so long how to get them out, finally,

Suzy's mom screamed, "We've been thinking for almost an hour and we will not give up. I just got an idea that might work. We can take a sharp and heavy object like an axe or a hammer that can help us open the door. But I'm sorry Niola as we'll have to break your house property, i.e., the antenna room's door." Niola screamed from the other side of the door, "Oh please, please don't about that. We are stuck in here for so long and we desperately need a way out. I really don't care about what happens to the door, just help us!!!"

The wooden door broke in no time and both of them sighed in relief, finally leaving the dusty and old antenna. After they got out everyone started questioning them on how, when and why all these scenarios took place. They were tensed after getting out, but Jiya remembered that the translator and the radio receiver were still connected to the antenna.

She ran to get it but just then a strong wind blew the wire and sparks started flying. She was terrified. Immediately, when the wind stopped, all the spooky weather went back to as it was before. Everyone huddled and was surprised to see such a fast difference in the weather. Suzy exclaimed, "This should've been recorded in the Guinness World Record as it's the first time the weather god became happy so fast! By the way, what's that translator for?" The translator sent a beeping sound and as soon as Jiya approached the translator, to her surprise something really unique was written and by reading the output of the translation, she gasped in disbelief. Everyone saw her expression and created a commotion on seeing what was translated, so to not set fire to the crowd, Niola decided to read the whole paragraph so that everyone wouldn't have to waste on reading. She then snatched the device from Jiya's hand and read aloud.

"Uhh-umm, so let me read what made Jiya gasp in such disbelief. So it says, Activate call mode, activate call mode. "Emergency, emergency, emergency!!!" This made everyone look at each other in surprise. Nobody knew what was happening and some also said that the translator might be incorrect as it was old, so trash it. But Jiya was stuck with her thoughts, saying, "A, R, I, M. Hmmm... I think the code word that was written on that board must be related to this translation. Well indeed, I too think that the translation is just rubbish but on the other hand, my father told me that no matter how old the translator is, no matter how rubbish and stupid the generated translation might be, no translator is ever wrong. Find out a way and you'll definitely succeed ahead, just keep on doing trial and error after trial and error, but don't ever lose hope.

We'll have to find some way or the other way to decode the message from Mars and if we find it we will be awarded to work with NASA on an internship and also host our very own kids space program where we'll be the leaders. I can't wait for that moment to happen, Yahoo!!!" The father shed tears of joy after seeing his daughter implement the things he taught.

'A, R, I, M'- this code was wandering in everyone's minds, what could it mean and the translation to that should also be related with the code word. But no matter what, everyone put pressure on their soft brains and nobody could get an answer. Just like we solve an equation of finding the value of x, but it was a way more difficult than that. Thinking, thinking, the time passed by but the answer to the acronym was of no avail. It showed 1 am on the clock but nobody slept, instead they lent a hand to Jiya by thinking of the code word. Suzy smiled and glanced at the stars, everyone saw her reaction and filled their hearts to hope for the answer, she asserted, "I got the first two letters of the code, A, stands for a, and R, stands for a robot. Now listen carefully to my logic, since we got a weird translation of the words saying emergency and umm... activate call mode. That truly signifies that only a robot can call for help with such signals and this robot is somewhere lost on Mars, right?" Everyone clapped loudly with a lot of enthusiasm and absolutely believed in what Suzy asserted.

Jiya exclaimed in excitement, "I too got the letters for the last two words, as Suzy said that it might be lost on Mars, so I, stands for is, and, M, stands for missing!!!" Each and everyone present there jumped in excitement for solving out the code word. Both Suzy and Jiya felt proud for explaining the code word and indeed, they were hundred percent right. What a blissful news it was! However, they were only halfway there. Unfortunately, they were left to find where, why and how a robot can be missing on Mars (a not so well-known planet by the scientists, astronauts or the astrologers). But, one true desire stuck like glue in Jiya's heart and it was that, "I will one day, definitely find the exact and precise message from Mars and will never say, 'NO' to accomplishing this wondrous task given by the mighties [God to Jiya]. I will never let go of my dream, never ever!!!" The family rushed to the scientists to tell them how clever their daughters are in figuring out secret codes. After they arrived Jiya and Suzy told the scientist what they decoded - "Oh how excellent that you all are present here! We would like to tell you that it's time we start working with you to figure out the entire message. Basically, the code word you told us to solve is solved. 'A' stands for A, 'R' stands for robot, 'I' stands for is and 'M' stands for missing. So, all together it forms a sentence- 'A robot is missing'."

After hearing the kids, two scientists started making fun of them, "Ha ha, so funny! We really like your make-up sentence. 'A robot is missing!' How could it be really possible, 'Little Scientists'. Ha ha ha ha!!!"

The two girls got angry and spoke up, "Excuse me, 'Big Scientists'! Whatever we thought while building this sentence was based on proper analysis and logic. If you want to hear it we are always ready to explain, ok?" The two scientists looked at each other in a funny way, they then again laughed and exclaimed, "Ha ha! We don't like listening to boring and illogical discussions, so keep those 'Proper analysis and Proper logic' with you only, tucked in your pockets!"

One of the scientists stated, "Wow! I believe you two are so good at decoding secret codes, but it's time we'll have to give you some advice. See, the way you are helping us is excellent, however, we are highly trained professionals and along with that we are scientists. You guys tell me, are scientists supposed to work without help, or rely on non-scientist people, especially like you tiny tots? Now it's time to stop helping us. What you had to do you have done already. Please don't help us with anything more. We're capable enough to solve messages independently. Also, you might lead us to an error as you both are just school kids.

Focus on your studies first then when you both get a job, become a scientist, doctor, engineer or whatever you want. Then you'll have the ability to make your own decisions or solve messages.

So, don't ever think of lending us a hand, because we are well-known and professionals in our work." However, after hearing this from the scientists, the little girls were extremely disappointed to see how easily the scientists underestimated their power to reach the top.

They decided only amongst them, that they would solve the message on their own and not include the scientists in their plan.

ELEVEN

A Mysterious Discovery

After they reached their house with sadness and discouragement, everyone slept on their beds disappointedly. Soon, time flew within hours and the rooster woke everyone up, "I wonder, how will today's day pass? I hope for some new and innovative discoveries... But wait, where's everyone?" Jiya yawned.

She was in total astonishment as nobody was present. She moved her head from left to right but didn't even find a shadow. With curiosity, she jumped off her bed and walked towards her parents' room. No one. She walked towards Suzy's family's room, no one. She then finally approached Niola's room but surprisingly, all rooms were empty.

She got a bit scared and imagined herself in a horror story; she got goosebumps and got even more scared. Unfortunately, there was no sign of anyone in the house, poor Jiya felt lonely but had a bit of hope that still showed her light to the gate of success. With the help of that gate, she called her parents. As soon as she called, it said that their phone was switched off. It did not matter who she dialled, everyone's phones were switched off.

Now the horror began, she got afraid and stressfully ran to her room. She grabbed a pillow and a blanket and hid in it, squishing it up. She contacted almost a million times but there was no answer, until someone rang the doorbell loud and furious, "Dinggg, donggg, dinggg, donggg!!!"

The scared girl thought twice to answer the door and with her fingers crossed, she opened it. To her surprise, a mailman was standing. He asked the young lady if he could get his money back as her parents had left somewhere. She bravely put a question to the mailman, "Left somewhere, what do you mean by left somewhere???" He replied, "Well dear, aren't you aware?

Few hours before, the six people in your house were taken by two-three scientists in a vintage blue car. I don't exactly remember the number plate but I do know that the starting digit was 7 and the ending one was 6. So, they told me they'll return my money back within an hour but now it's too late, do you have the money?" She happily answered, "I surely do not have the money but what I surely know is that you have a car. Right?" The man said yes, then Jiya shouted, "Then let's follow that vintage car!!!"

The man became speechless but did the same thing the girl said. He started the ignition of his car and sped the car at full speed. Jiya got happy as soon as she heard about her parents, with that happiness all over the way, they reached NASA's radio signal point. He exclaimed, "They might be here..." Both of them got down and went inside. Jiya screamed and ran, "Mommy, daddy!" She got excited as she saw her parents right over there.

Her parents saw her, and hugged her tightly. They told their daughter why they left her alone, "See Jiya, actually at 4 in the morning we received a call from the scientists and surprisingly they got to know that we decoded their code word correctly. They brought us here immediately and because children weren't allowed to come, Suzy, who was also sleeping, had been in the car but we thought not to wake you up after such an exhausting day. So, we left you alone at home." Jiya understood their compulsion easily. In no time, the scientists appeared and asked Jiya of how she got access there, but they allowed her inside the radio transceiver room. Soon, the scientists set up a wide discussion about the Mars message, "Didn't we tell you to not help us by finding out anything. What's the matter now, do you think we're fools to be telling you all this.

Don't ever come to us, this is our first and last warning!" The kids sadly returned back to their home and they started researching in almost all websites for any such consequence but couldn't find out the answer to the code word. Unexpectedly, they found a website that told about a very intelligent robot in the early 2000's. Suzy ignored it and started scrolling down but Jiya stopped her and scrolled back up. There was a whole page saying that a robot was the most intelligent robot at that time. It also explained that whenever that robot used to sense danger, it used to generate a sound saying

'Emergency'. That was the exact thing they got translated as. But how could that article be related to the current situation? But what would that robot be doing on Mars since years and till date nobody rescued it? Also, the robot, if it would've been rescued secretly, then that's extremely strange. Now it all depends on those two smart kids that would have to figure out, if that is real or not real, and then what to plan next?

TWELVE
The Robot on Mars

Jiya asked Suzy, "What do you think, Suzy? Should we focus on this part of the article now?" Suzy paused, seemingly lost in thought and zoning out. Noticing her friend's lack of interest, Jiya started scrolling further. But just then, Suzy stopped her, agreeing with the idea. The two friends exchanged smiles, refocusing on the article together. This moment captured the essence of their friendship: even though Suzy wasn't interested at first, she valued Jiya's enthusiasm. Jiya felt grateful to have such a supportive friend, and soon, they both began jotting down calculations in their notebooks.

Just then, Niola came to check on them, and Jiya stood up, saying, "Maybe we can work on this tonight. But for now, let's have lunch." As Niola led them downstairs, the doorbell rang.

She opened the door to the mailman and received a letter. Curiously examining it, she handed it to the girls, saying, "This is strange – the mail's addressed to both of you. Could it be from the scientists?" Suzy's eyes widened with excitement, "Oh, we've been waiting for this!" The letter read, "Our scientists have made a very intriguing discovery. We'd be delighted to invite you to the planetarium – please come as soon as you can!"

The two best friends exchanged thrilled glances, quickly asking their parents for permission. In no time, they were on their way to the planetarium. Upon arrival, they were greeted warmly, "Welcome to our planetarium! Prepare to be amazed by our extraordinary discovery." Rushing in, they were astonished to find it was just like the content in the article. Suzy mentioned this to one of the scientists, who, though skeptical, acknowledged their insight, saying, "It sounds unlikely, but you both must have sharp minds if you caught onto this. You must have done some research yourselves!" Jiya and Suzy beamed with pride.

Then, one of the scientists mentioned a puzzling radio signal. "We have a translator that might help us decode it," he began, but Jiya interrupted, "We already figured that out! Now, we just need to understand why a robot would be stranded on Mars." Surprised by their knowledge, the scientist felt a bit embarrassed. As the team gathered to discuss the documentary, it became clear that nobody had been able to make sense of it. They suspected it contained outdated information and decided not to waste any more time on it. However, Jiya and Suzy were determined and resolved to keep researching until they uncovered the truth.

The scientists tried to dissuade the girls from spending more time on it, but they wouldn't be swayed. Back home, Niola cautioned them, "I appreciate your hard work, but don't you think there are other things you could focus on? The scientists have moved on, and you could, too." Suzy replied firmly, "I understand, Aunty Niola, but we're not like everyone else. Thinking outside the box is our speciality.

We refuse to quit halfway through; giving up just isn't in our vocabulary." Niola smirked, replying, "Those are big words. Show me, and then I'll believe you."

Although nobody else had faith in them, the girls resolved to prove everyone wrong. They knew that researching robots stuck on Mars was challenging, but they were driven by a dream to finish what they'd started.

THIRTEEN

The Collaborative Quest

Unexpectedly, a sentence caught both of the kids' attention. The information outweighed every other discovery, but it took plenty of time to research it. That extraordinary sentence was the name of the company that sent a spaceship. The only valuable information provided on the entire page of the company article was, "A spaceship sent three people to research on Mars, and along with them, there was a robot as well...so now the robot is missing!"

Upon reading this, Jiya and Suzy's minds sought a conclusion on what was going on. After a while, Suzy told Jiya to get something from the other room. Jiya being lost in thought denied the request, so Suzy went all by herself saying that she wanted her favourite thing now; Jiya was clueless but still focused on what could be the conclusion of such a sentence. Within a flash,

Suzy arrived back with a box filled with tasty popcorn. Jiya questioned what the popcorn was for. Suzy genuinely answered, "I thought the sentence was interesting, so for me, when I see something interesting, the only thing that comes to my mind is a movie, and thus movie = popcorn time! So I brought popcorn for both of us. Bon appétit 'BFF'!" Suzy then stuffed popcorn in her mouth and handed over the leftovers to her bestie. Jiya chuckled after observing her innocence and took some of the popcorn as well.

After both of them feasted on the popcorn, Jiya threw the box in the dustbin and leaned towards the computer, she uttered, "Now this seems way harder than we thought." Suzy continued, "Exactly, I too think that this sentence is only leading us to confusion. Let the robot stay on Mars as he wants, nobody has to care." With sparkling eyes and a majestic smile on Jiya's face, she came up with a conclusion, "Suzy, you're god, you're an angel, you solved the confusion!" Suzy speechlessly looked at Jiya.

She thought that Jiya was talking nonsense, but then Jiya continued, "You said that the robot is staying on Mars and nobody has to care about it. Didn't we see that the article was made years ago? Could it be that the three astronauts who travelled to Mars to discover something unique, upon entering Mars's atmosphere, miscalculated the low gravitational force and crashed!?...and the robot that they were travelling with, being a machine, some of its parts might have separated away from the crash. That robot could have crashed on Mars! ...and... The NASA scientists must have been relying on the robot to know the astronauts' condition but like I said, the robot must have crashed elsewhere when the craft and its crew were lost and that's how they lost track of the robot and the crew!" Jiya ended with a sigh of relief and huffed.

Suzy picked up the threads when Jiya got tired, "Therefore, the scientist must have not reached any conclusion after years of trying to figure out where the tracking could've been lost and decided to create a new spaceship to research on other planets, as Mars[for the scientists] might be too dangerous without vital information. And ever since we received the signal again, the scientists thought about researching it again but they gave that up as well." With enthusiasm, Jiya exclaimed, "Wouldn't that make us, 'A Special Scientist'!" The way both of them thought this was extraordinary, showed their passion for discovering the unknown. When Niola entered their room, she said, "Looks like you both aren't ready to give up, come on, it's just going to waste your time. Anyways you guys showed your love towards science, you guys got invited by the scientists and also you guys got the chance to decode the code. What else do you want in life?" Both of them said together, "Recognition!"

Niola was left being tongue-tied. She then said arrogantly, "Go ahead, 'Little Scientists', keep working. One day you'll realize that I was right. When you both give up, don't come filled with regret for not listening to me. You can continue your work till night or till whatever time you want, I just came here to mention that you might soon regret what you wasted your time on. Please work, continue your work, 'Little Scientists'."

Both the tiny-tots chuckled and then Suzy told Niola, "Well, there is no future where we'll come to say that 'we regret not heeding your advice'". Jiya added, "Because we already found out what you claimed we'll regret." Niola was in total surprise because she didn't ever think in her dreams that her 'Little Scientists' would work so hard to achieve their most fascinating goal. Jiya and Suzy exclaimed together, "Never underestimate your 'Little Scientists' hard work and power!!!" After hearing such enthusiastic power from her nieces, Niola for a second blossomed with pride. She asked her nieces to tell what they figured out in conclusion. Both of them narrated the entire story to their aunt and at the end they saw their parents were standing at their room's door, listening to all the conversation they had from the beginning.

Suzy and Jiya felt proud after discovering the message. Suzy's mom verbalised, "Oh you two, why are you so proud and delighted just yet? I suggest practising those big smiles for the whole world to see, because, isn't an award ceremony remaining for us?" The whole family was in complete happiness for having two bright kids like Suzy and Jiya.

Jiya's dad took them to the car and drove off to the scientists in a rush. The family felt proud until they reached the scientists. Jiya and Suzy were jolly too, for discovering something special, something unknown to the world.

The scientists were astonished by the two kids, they were surprised to see that the two kids had figured out the whole scenario. The scientists then announced, "You both are so intelligent, you're the best scientists we ever met! We are so proud of you! Now let's start working together to find out how to rescue the robot from Mars." The car started its engine and everyone was happy and excited to start their new journey of rescuing the robot. The whole family felt happy and proud, they started their journey with a smile on their faces.

After a long journey, they reached the planetarium and started their work. Hours passed by, no one slept, everyone was so focused on their work, they just wanted to complete the task. After a whole day, they were tired but were happy for what they had discovered. They decided to go home and take rest, but before that, they had a small meeting. The scientists told the kids, "You both are the best, and we are so proud of you.

We'll never forget the help you did, and we'll surely give you both an award for helping us." The kids were on cloud nine, they were so happy that they felt they could fly. With that happiness, they left the planetarium and returned back to their home. They slept peacefully after having a tiring day. The next day, everyone woke up with a fresh mind and started their work again.

FOURTEEN

Triumph and Recognition

With our special thanks to Suzy and Jiya, we'd love to assign them the job of figuring out why a robot is missing on Mars. This might be a surprising statement for society to believe, but truth needs to be spoken. So, Jiya and Suzy, remember, never feel embarrassed by what society thinks, but be proud of yourselves for uncovering the truth. All the very best to both of you!

The scientists asserted this when the family came to the planetarium to present the evidence they had gathered. Both kids realized their thought processes and admiration for space technologies had grown, so they should start their own kids' space program, as mentioned in the award. Jiya asked the scientists, "So, where is our gift?"

The senior scientist laughingly answered, "No, no, no! First, we will have to go to the award ceremony, and then you, 'Little Scientists,' as you guys wanted, will gain recognition by facing the camera and being seen worldwide. After all this happens, you will be awarded your very own ticket to start your own kids' space programs every Sunday, along with an internship to participate in discussions on different space technologies. So, are you both excited?" The 'Little Scientists' exclaimed together, "Of course!" "Then let's get this party started, oh yeah, oh yeah!"

Happily, the scientists, Jiya's family, Suzy's family, and Aunt Niola headed off to a place where the scientists suggested going for the award ceremony. Jiya realized she needed to call her supporters in Seattle—the scientists Jiya found in the beginning who were like her coaches, helping her build the foundation of this entire project. She called them and said, "Thank you, thank you, thank you, thank you so much!!!

Only because of you, today I succeeded in this—" "Before you tell everything, let me tell you that hopefully we were aware of all this before. So we have a surprise for you!" interrupted the scientist on the phone. Jiya excitedly questioned, "What's the surprise? Will I get it when I come back to Seattle?

No, I want it now! Tell me, please!" The scientist on the other side of the phone responded, "Look at your back!" Jiya turned around and to her surprise, a group of scientists were gathered to hug Jiya tightly. That astonished her, and when she saw the scientist she was partnering with, she cried out, "None other than my one and only bestie or BFF, 'Suzy'!" The scientists congratulated Suzy gracefully, and by then, Jiya and Suzy had reached the place where the award ceremony was to be held. Due to such surprises coming one after another, Jiya lost track of her surroundings.

The area was filled with media people, with all the scientists sitting in a corner and the two 'Little Scientists' standing in the middle of the stage with the award presenter, who looked like a high-profile celebrity. The audience was sitting right in front of the stage, excitedly cheering for the two by presenting many loud applauses.

Jiya and Suzy were so happy they couldn't control their happiness and started laughing joyfully. The award presenter was Mr. Johnson. Along with him, his beloved wife, Mrs. Johnson, was also part of the award-giving team.

The couple then handed over the award, a phenomenal, golden trophy depicting Mars and a robot. The two kids took it with extreme pride, facing the media people who were taking their photos. Both families started to shed tears of joy. That moment was the most memorable time anyone could ever remember. The scientists gazed at that splendid view after seeing the little ones receive a startling trophy that caught everyone's attention. The video, taken by the media people, was going live, and more than 10 million people were watching it.

At last, Mr. Johnson gave a wonderful speech admiring both the kids and the audience, "Good morning, ladies and gentlemen! We all know why we gathered here today, of course you'll be wondering that we gathered here to appraise the two smart children and award them an internship for attending any discussions that will take place in any scientific research and a wondrous trophy.

Well, if you were wondering like this, I would say, you're 100% wrong. We not only came here to appraise them but also to provide them with recognition in front of society. I still remember when my grandfather once told me to never give up and to continue to work on what you were completing. I'm starting to think that these two youngsters were present with me when my grandfather was telling me all this, ha, ha, ha, ha!

So, this was all from my side, I just wanted to tell you both one thing, continue this till your future and keep on achieving recognition every day. God bless you both! And all the very best from all of us for the future and present as well, for carrying this heavy trophy in your car's trunk, ha, ha!" Everyone chuckled, including the two kids.

Jiya and Suzy beamed with pride. Overwhelmed with emotion, Suzy wiped away tears. "I can't believe it! We're getting an internship with NASA, starting our own kids' space program, and receiving this incredible trophy! Is this all a dream or for real?" Jiya cried, "No darling, it's for real!"

With all such incredible events taking place, the place was then filled with a delightful chaos of happiness and joy. Everybody lined up to take Jiya's and Suzy's signatures on their clothes. Some people got so mad that they rushed to the tattoo artist and requested them to make their signatures on their feet, back, and also on their forehead (that's weird). But with all that madness, it showed how much they respected their stunning work. The smart kiddos parents' reaction was unbelievable! They were proud of giving birth to such smart and clever children. From then on, everyone started to call Jiya and Suzy, 'Little Scientists'. Jiya unexpectedly grabbed the mic and announced, "So in conclusion, the mission, 'Message From Mars' is deciphered!!! Let's start the party!

FIFTEEN

Tick-Tock-Tick

After all this chaotic environment of happiness, the scientists told Jiya and Suzy to go to their car and head off to a special planetarium, keeping the heavy/bulky trophy in the car's trunk. They sent the location of that planetarium to Dad, who asked, "Umm... why are you sending the location of a special planetarium?"

One of the scientists responded, "As the award was an internship to work with us, NASA scientists, according to our calculations, you are welcome from today only to start giving some requirements that should be improvised, or we'll have an interesting topic to discuss on.

Also, since the award mentioned that you can open any space program and be the leader, we will have to discuss what to open, whom to invite, and where to do it.

So that's the reason we sent you the details of a big planetarium, where we can have a good conference." Jiya's dad nodded his head and started the car. Along with Dad, Jiya, Suzy,

Suzy's parents, Jiya's mom, and Aunt Niola paid their visit to the planetarium as well.

On the way, when everyone was sitting in their respective seats, a weird noise came from the car's trunk. At first, everyone ignored it, but it came again the second time. Jiya was curious, so she asked, "Dad? Can you stop the car for a minute, actually I want to check the car's trunk that's causing all this noise?" Jiya's dad replied, "Oh, actually there are many big and tall speed-breakers, and since the trophy is kept back, it might be moving because of the tall speed-breakers. So, there is no need to check on that." Jiya thought that her dad must be right, so she ignored it again.

But when she turned back, she saw a glimpse of a robotic hand that had popped up on its own. When she told the others in the car to see, they were all dumbfounded. Jiya wondered, "How can we see a robotic hand here? This is really impossible!

The only thing that was kept in the car's trunk was a trophy. But wait a second, how can it be that the robot that was discovered on Mars came back here when the scientists did not rescue that robot.

Or did that robot arrive on Earth with the help of aliens!? No, that's really illogical. Would that robot be helpful for our planet or really dangerous and harm us as well? But how did a robot that was stuck on Mars for years reach here when nobody even thought of it or rescued it? If it would've been rescued secretly, then that's extremely strange. This robotic hand is leaving me clueless, how can it be? Wait, but what if that's really the same robot that we read and researched on, came to 'Life'?"

www.ingramcontent.com/pod-product-compliance
Lightning Source LLC
LaVergne TN
LVHW041539070526
838199LV00046B/1734